THE NEW ADVENTURES
of MOTHER GOOSE

GENTLE RHYMES FOR HAPPY TIMES

CREATED BY
BRUCE LANSKY

ILLUSTRATED BY
STEPHEN CARPENTER

Meadowbrook Press
Distributed by Simon & Schuster
New York

Library of Congress Cataloging-in-Publication Data

Lansky, Bruce
    The new adventures of Mother Goose: gentle rhymes for happy times/created by Bruce Lansky;
    illustrated by Stephen Carpenter.
         p.   cm.
    Summary: A collection of contemporary Mother Goose rhymes, based on the
  original characters.
    1. Mother Goose–Parodies, imitations, etc.   2. Children's poetry, American.
      [1. Nursery rhymes.   2. American poetry.]
I. Carpenter, Stephen, ill.   II. Title.
PS3562.A564N48 1993
811'.54–dc20   93-11129
                                             CIP
                                           AC

ISBN: 0-88166-201-1
Simon & Schuster #: 0-671-87288-5

Managing Editor: Elizabeth H. Weiss
Editorial Coordinator: Cathy Broberg
Production Manager: Kate Laing
Desktop Publishing Coordinator: Jon C. Wright
Designer: Tabor Harlow
Production Artist: Erik Broberg

Published by Meadowbrook Press, 18318 Minnetonka Boulevard, Deephaven, MN 55391.

BOOK TRADE DISTRIBUTION by Simon & Schuster, a division of Simon and Schuster, Inc., 1230
Avenue of the Americas, New York, NY 10020.

98 97 96 95 94   6 5 4

Printed in the United States of America

We would like to thank the teachers and students of the following kindergarten and preschool classrooms for taking time to help us select the poems for this collection. Your enthusiasm for this project has made it all the more worthwhile: Ann Adams, Blake School; Bessie Arne, Children's Workshop; Sally Budroot, Marlyce Erickson, and Kathy Pope, Groveland Elementary; Gene Ford, St. Margaret Mary Learning Center; Paige Frondell, Kids & Company; Richard Gosen, Wayzata Learning Center; Leah Grove, Turtle Lake Elementary; Dawn Hansen, Kids & Company; Irma Kelley, Orono Primary School; Cathy Kinee, Hope Daycare; Terry Laden, Hopkins Montessori; Jody Hlavka and Carol Wald, Kids' Art Studio; Tracey Orr, Peter Hobart School; Diane Schimelpfenig, Tanglen Elementary; Judy Spenser, Fulton Elementary; Linda Stewart, Deephaven Learning Center; Jana Rasmussen, St. David's Elementary; Jeanine Wanberg, Minnetonka Montessori; Nancy Burton Wiederhold, Deephaven Montessori; Eden Prairie Children's World; Eden Prairie KinderCare; Eden Prairie New Horizon Child Care; and Minnetonka Children's World.

Special thanks to the many parents and teachers who reviewed the manuscript, including: Jane Al-Tamimi, Polly Andersen, Kathryn Bartee, Jim and Bonnie Bohen, Ralph and Katie Dayton, Gary and Mary Elling, Mary Mackey Faulkner, Larry Holgerson, Marsha Jacobson, Doug and Catherine Kelley, Vicki McKinney, Kelsey Bush Nadear, Steve Sobieniak, Frank and Julie Stieve, Janice Surian, Linda Torres, Jon and Mary Wright, and many others.

CONTENTS

Old Mother Goose	*Bruce Lansky*	4
Mary Had a Little Jam	*Bruce Lansky*	5
Hickory, Dickory, Dock	*Jeffery Goodson*	6
Hickory, Dockory, Hic	*Bob Zanger*	6
There Was a Little Girl	*Brad Schreiber*	7
Georgie Porgie	*Bruce Lansky*	7
Little Miss Muffet	*Bruce Lansky*	8
Jack and Jill	*Bruce Lansky*	9
Jack Was Nimble	*Bruce Lansky*	10
Little Bo-Peep	*Bruce Lansky*	11
Little Boy Blue	*Bruce Lansky*	11
Diddle Diddle, Dumpling, My Girl June	*Bruce Lansky*	12
Diddle Diddle, Dumpling, My Son Scooter	*Gwen Molnar*	12
Row, Row, Row Your Boat	*Bruce Lansky*	13
Rub-a-Dub-Dub	*Mary Collins Dunne*	14
London Bridge	*Bruce Lansky*	14
Humpty Dumpty	*Gwen Molnar*	15
Mary, Mary, Quite Contrary	*Bruce Lansky*	16
Tom, Tom, the Teacher's Son	*Sylvia Andrews*	16
Old Mother Hubbard	*Bruce Lansky*	17
Peter, Peter, Sugar Eater	*Bruce Lansky*	18
Fee Fie Fo Fum	*Bruce Lansky*	19
Hiccup, Hiccup	*Bruce Lansky*	19
Some Like It Hot	*Bruce Lansky*	19
Hey Diddle, Diddle	*Stan Lee Werlin*	20
Lavender Blue	*Bruce Lansky*	21
Old King Cole	*Larry Cohen & Steve Zweig*	21
Pat a Cake	*Bruce Lansky*	22
Pat a Pie	*Virginia Kroll*	22
There Was an Old Woman	*Larry Cohen & Steve Zweig*	23
Yankee Doodle	*Robert Scotellaro*	24
Roses Are Red	*Bruce Lansky*	25
Jack Sprat	*Lois Muehl*	26
Simple Simon	*Bruce Lansky*	26
Wee Willie Winkie	*Bruce Lansky*	27
Dapple-Gray	*Brad Schreiber*	28
Three Kind Mice	*Robert Scotellaro*	29
Sweetheart, You're My Little Star	*Bruce Lansky*	30
Twinkle, Twinkle, Little Star	*Elizabeth Weiss*	30
Star Light, Star Bright	*Bruce Lansky*	31
Rock-a-Bye, Baby	*Bruce Lansky*	32

Old Mother Goose
     used to fly through the air,
riding a gander—
     they made a fine pair.

Now when she wants
     to get somewhere soon,
she rides on the cow
     that jumped over the moon.

Mary had a little jam;
    she spread it on a waffle.
And if she hadn't eaten ten,
    she wouldn't feel so awful.

Hickory, dickory, dock,
   a mouse jumped in my sock.
He wiggled his nose
   and tickled my toes,
which gave me quite a shock!

Hickory, dockory, hic,
   the day your clock gets sick,
and says, "Tock Tick,"
   but not, "Tick Tock,"
call the Hickory Dickory Doc.

There was a little girl, and she had a little curl
   that drooped in the middle of her face.
To improve her view, she took some goo
   and stuck it back in place.

Georgie Porgie, what a shame
   kids call you such a silly name.
Now I think you know it's true
   that teasing isn't nice to do.

CALL ME GEORGE

Little Miss Muffet
    sat on a tuffet,
licking an ice-cream cone.
    Along came a spider,
who dangled beside her—
    she told him to go get his own.

Jack and Jill
    went down a hill
in a fast toboggan.
    They hit a bump,
which made a lump
    in the middle of Jack's noggin.

Jack was nimble.
Jack was quick.
Jack jumped over
the candlestick.

Jack kept jumping,
much too close.
Now his pants
smell like burnt toast.

Little Bo-Peep throws her clothes in a heap,
which makes her room one giant mess.
And when she wakes up, she calls for her pup
to hunt through the heap for her dress.

Little Boy Blue,
   stop blowing your horn.
You'll wake up the neighbors;
   it's two in the morn!
You've got to be quiet
   so people can sleep.
Get under your covers
   and start counting sheep.

Diddle diddle, dumpling, my girl June,
eats her lunch without a spoon.
She's a mess from head to toe—
so in the bathtub she must go.

Diddle diddle, dumpling, my son Scooter,
played around with my computer.
He pressed the buttons, he hit the keys,
and now it only prints Chinese.

HOW NOW
BROWN
COW

12

Row, row, row your boat,
gently 'round the lake.
Don't stand up and rock the boat—
that's a big mistake.

Rub-a-dub-dub,
   three men in a tub,
and what do you think they said?
   "Too crowded, we fear,
let's get out of here,
   and each take a shower instead."

London Bridge is falling down,
   falling down, falling down.
There's no way to walk to town.
   Take the ferry.

Humpty Dumpty sat on a wall.
    Humpty Dumpty had a great fall.
I wish they'd had super glue way back then—
    they could have put Humpty together again.

Mary, Mary, quite contrary,
what does your garden grow:
spinach, broccoli, cauliflower?
To which Mary answered, "No!"

Lollipops

Jelly Beans

Tom, Tom, the teacher's son,
went to school when he was one.
The only thing young Tom could do
was play a game of peekaboo.

RECYCLE
SAVE THE
EARTH

Old Mother Hubbard
    went to the cupboard
to get her poor dog a bone.
    But the dog couldn't wait,
so when dinner was late,
    he ordered a pizza by phone.

PIZZA-2-GO

17

Peter, Peter, sugar eater,
  always wanted food much sweeter.
Adding sugar was a blunder—
  now he is a toothless wonder.

SUGAR FLAKIES

A TRUNKFUL OF SWEET TASTE!

NEW! 75% MORE SUGAR

Fee Fie Fo Fum,
  I smell a pack of bubble gum.
Fee Fie Fo Fum,
  look out bubbles, here I come!

Hiccup, hiccup, go away!
  Don't come back another day.

Some like it hot,
  some like it cold,
  but oatmeal tastes yucky
    when it's nine days old.

Hey diddle, diddle,
    this rhyme is a riddle:
Can a cow fly over the moon?
    I bet you'll say, "No,"
but the answer is, "Yes"—
    if she's riding a hot-air balloon.

Lavender blue, rosemary green,
    when I am the king, you'll be the queen.
We'll sit on thrones, crowns on our heads.
    No one will send us up to our beds.

Old King Cole
    was a chubby old soul
who loved to play the fiddle.
    When given a chance,
    he'd often dance
        till his pants split down the middle.

Pat a cake, pat a cake, baker Sue,
  bake me a cake that says, "I love you."
I've saved up my money; I'm ready to pay—
  I'll give it to Mommy on Valentine's Day.

Pat a pie, pat a pie, baker Dan,
  bake me a pizza as fast as you can.
Knead it, and roll it, and spread on the cheese.
  Then sprinkle on pepper; I'll try not to sneeze.

There was an old woman who lived in a shoe,
which wasn't too bad when the winter winds blew.
But the strong summer sun was too hot to handle,
so she packed up her stuff and moved to a sandal.

Yankee Doodle went to town,
    riding on a rooster.
His saddle wasn't high enough,
    so now he's got a booster.

Roses are red,
   violets are blue;
I wish I could ride
   on a big kangaroo.

Roses are red,
   violets are blue;
I wish I could ride
   on a dinosaur, too.

Jack Sprat would have no cat,
his wife would have no dog.
So when they went to buy a pet,
they settled on a hog.

Simple Simon met a snowman
standing with a broom.
"I'll give you fifty cents," he said,
"if you'll clean up my room."

Wee Willie Winkie ran down all the stairs,
   hugging a blanket and two teddy bears.
"I can't fall asleep," he cried as he ran.
   "Look under my bed! There's a bogeyman!"

         His father carried him up to his room.
            He turned on the light, then searched for a broom.
         He swept out some stuff from under the bed—
            two slippers, a bone, and Willie's dog, Fred.

I had a little pony,
  his name was Dapple-Gray.
I lent him to a woman
  whose horse was sick one day.
But rain came down in showers
  and made puddles on the ground.
My pony got so muddy,
  I called him Dapple-Brown.

Three kind mice, see how they run!
  They all ran after the farmer's wife,
they took out some cheese,
  and they cut her a slice.
Did you ever see such a sight in your life
  as three kind mice?

Sweetheart, you're my little star.
How I love the way you are.
How I wonder what you'll be,
as I bounce you on my knee.

Twinkle, twinkle, little star,
how I wonder why you are
shining down on me so bright—
please watch over me tonight.

Star light, star bright,
first star I see tonight,
I'm going to try with all my might
to keep my jammies dry all night.

Rock-a-bye, baby, on the treetop.
  When the wind blows, the cradle will rock;
when the birds sing, the baby will smile,
  and fall asleep happy in a short while.